Young Dracula

&

Young Monsters

by

Michael Lawrence

Illustrated by Chris Mould

You do not need to read this page – just get on with the book!

Young Dracula first published in 2002 in Great Britain
Young Monsters first published in 2003 in Great Britain

Published in one volume as *Young Dracula & Young Monsters* in 2006 in Great Britain by Barrington Stoke

ISBN-10: 1-84299-445-X
ISBN-13: 978-1-84299-445-0

Printed in Great Britain by Bell & Bain Ltd

Young Dracula

by

Michael Lawrence

Illustrated by Chris Mould

For Megan Larkin,
my greatest critic

Contents

Chapter 1
Wilfred the Bold

I'm sure you've heard of Count Dracula, the evil vampire who could turn himself into a bat at will. The creepy fellow who always dressed in black and preferred a neckful of warm blood to a mug of milky tea any day.

Yes, everyone's heard of Count Dracula. But how many of us know what he was like when young? Before he grew tall, swept his

hair back, and started hanging round graveyards? Not many of us! And why? Because until now, the story of young Dracula has been a well-kept secret – a secret that I (a very nosy writer) have at last unearthed.

Before I tell you this secret story, however, you must learn something of life at Castle Dracula before the lad was born. Pay attention now. This bit's important.

In a remote corner of Transylvania, there were once two rival vampires. One was Count Dracula, the other Baron Gertler. The Count and the Baron lived in tall, black castles on opposite sides of the valley.

Far below, between the two castles, there was a village.

Every night, very late, village bloodmen (the Transylvanian version of milkmen) rode up to the castles with bottles of fresh blood for the Count and the Baron. The bloodmen collected a cupful from everyone in the village between the ages of ten and eighty. The villagers had no choice in this.

Give blood freely or
the vampire lords will
come for it themselves
and take it from the neck,
which is painful

Now, Count Dracula and Baron Gertler
were the last of their line. Neither of them
had children to follow in their bloody
footsteps. But one year, the Count brought
home a wife, and the following year Countess
Dracula gave birth to a son, whom they
called Wilfred.

When Baron Gertler heard that the
Draculas had an heir, he became very
jealous. He turned himself into a giant bat,
flew to the castle across the valley, and
snatched the babe from his mother's arms
while the Count was clipping his toenails in
the bath. Then he flew off with the child
under his arm.

The distressed Countess rushed to the
window to save her darling son, but reaching
for him she leant out too far and tumbled
to her death far below. Her scream brought
the Count dripping from the bath.

As soon as he saw what had happened, the Count ground his vampire teeth with rage, turned himself into a bat, and flew after the Baron. The Baron escaped, but the Count managed to save baby Wilfred and bring him home.

Some nights later, the Count sneaked into Castle Gertler before the Baron was up, and hammered a wooden stake through his mean old heart.

Twelve years passed. Count Dracula was now half the vampire he had been. He was lame and could no longer turn himself into a bat. He never went out at night. The villagers no longer feared him, and the bloodmen no longer delivered. He had to content himself with the blood of the rats that scampered around the castle.

One dark and miserable midnight, the old Count sat gazing out from his high tower. On the hill across the valley stood the crumbling ruin of Castle Gertler. No-one had lived there since the Baron's death.

"Ah, those were the nights," the Count sighed, with a tear in his eye.

He missed having a real enemy. He missed being young and fit enough to go out for a neck or two of human blood when the fancy took him. There wasn't even anyone to talk to now. No-one that mattered anyway. It was no use talking to Wilfred. They had nothing in common, nothing at all.

"Are you all right, Father?"

The Count jumped. He hadn't heard Wilfred come up the stairs. "Oh, it's you," he snapped. "What do you want?"

Wilfred was worried about the old vampire. He was a kind and sensitive lad.

"I was wondering if you'd like a bowl of toad and tomato soup, Father."

The Count scowled. "No, Wilfred, I do not want soup. I want blood, gently warmed, bit of froth on top, no sugar. If you had any thought for your poor old father you'd go down to the valley, drag a villager out of bed, and drain his blood into a jug for me."

"But Father, I hate doing that, you know I do."

"To think," the Count said, "that one day you'll be head of the House of Dracula. Why, I wouldn't be surprised if the first thing you do when I'm turned to dust is put up pretty curtains and put flowers everywhere. You're not a vampire, Wilfred, you're a wimpire!"

Wilfred was badly stung by these harsh words. He so wanted to be like all the

Draculas before him. Was it *his* fault that he was different? He went down to his room and climbed into his coffin, where he tossed and turned sadly for a while.

At last he fell asleep. Wilfred had always had trouble keeping awake at night – another thing that upset his father. The Count was old-fashioned. He believed that vampires should sleep during the day and be up all night, sipping the red stuff.

The good thing about sleeping at night, from Wilfred's point of view, was the dreams. Night dreams were sweeter than day dreams. Tonight, for instance, he dreamt that he didn't have to live in a cold and gloomy castle or file his teeth at coffin-time.

In the dream, he didn't feel a wimp for preferring milk to blood either. He had a cow all of his own.

Lying beneath her in the straw and dung, he could drink fresh, warm milk to his heart's content.

In this wonderful dream, Wilfred ran through open fields in broad daylight, singing at the top of his voice. Sunlight didn't make him cry out in pain the moment it touched his skin, as it would in real life. In the dream, he was the Wilfred he longed to be.

But when he woke, the dream vanished and the gloom of the Castle settled about him once more. The Count's unkind remark came back to him: *"You're not a vampire, Wilfred, you're a wimpire."*

Wilfred sighed. "I so want Father to be proud of me," he said, and resolved to go out and prove that he was a true vampire after all.

He waited indoors all that day, hiding from the sunlight which would do him no good at all. Then, as night fell yet again, Wilfred, heir to the noble House of Dracula, slipped out of the castle. He took with him a jug to bring back his father's favourite tipple: human blood.

Wolves howled in the distance as Wilfred went down Bram Hill. He trembled, but on he went, down and down into the valley. He had no idea that his life was about to change – forever.

Chapter 2
Followed!

It was Wilfred's plan to go to the village. The villagers would be asleep at this hour, and with luck he would be able to tiptoe into cottage after cottage and take all the blood he needed from the necks of his victims without waking anyone. It was a suck and spit job.

Unfortunately, he had to pass through Stoker Wood to get to the village. No-one entered Stoker Wood at night unless they were either a vampire or very stupid indeed.

The trees in the wood creaked a lot, even though there was no wind. Unseen birds fluttered in the treetops above his head. Small creatures scurried and scuttled round his feet. Larger beasts moved about in the darkness, their eyes glowing like sly torches.

Wilfred gulped, but he gripped his jug all the more firmly, and on he went, deeper and deeper into the wood. He looked neither right nor left for fear of what he might see.

He'd been walking for about fifteen minutes when he noticed a small, regular sound some way behind him.

Padda-pad. Padda-pad. Padda-pad.

Wilfred paused. The small, regular sound paused too.

He began walking again.

Padda-pad. Padda-pad. Padda-pad.

He broke into a run. The small, regular sound also speeded up.

Padda-padda, padda-padda, padda-padda, pad.

And then? Wilfred tripped over a root and fell flat on his face.

And another sound joined the first.

Pant-pant-panta-pant. Pant-pant-panta-pant.

The hair on Wilfred's head sprang up, and so did he. To his feet, he sprang, and climbed the nearest tree until he reached a sturdy branch. His heart thudded madly as he looked down. An enormous wolf stood at the foot of the tree, staring up at him, licking its hairy lips.

"Ha!" jeered Wilfred. "Fooled you, Mr Wolf! You won't have *me* for supper tonight!"

He clapped his hands at his own cleverness. As he clapped, his elbow nudged something. Something big. Something with hot breath and wide, yellow eyes. Wilfred stopped clapping. He peered into the darkness.

On the branch, very near him, was a large, inky shape. What was it? For all he knew it was some wild creature that longed for a tasty snack of boy meat.

"Waaaaaaaaaaaaaaaaaaah!"

This was the sound Wilfred made as he toppled off the branch and fell into a pile of leaves. At the very feet of the wolf. The wolf growled hungrily – and pounced.

But as the wolf pounced, something odd happened. It should have torn Wilfred apart and swallowed his heart in a single gulp, but it did nothing of the kind. After pouncing on him, it simply lay there, on top of him, quite still, moving neither tooth nor muscle, ear or paw.

Wilfred, eyes firmly closed, lay beneath the heavy, unmoving wolf for some time expecting the worst. But when the worst didn't happen, he opened his eyes and prodded the beast gently.

"Mr Wolf, are you all right? Wolf? Nice wolfy."

Still the wolf did not move, so Wilfred eased himself out from under it. The wolf continued to lie there. This wasn't surprising, really, because there was an arrow in its back.

The wolf was as dead as a rusty doornail.

Chapter 3
The Night Hunter

Wilfred looked about him. Nothing moved. Nothing made a sound.

"H-h-h-hello?"

No reply. Not a word. Not a whisper. Not a burp.

Wilfred's spine tingled. The absolute silence and stillness worried him just as much as the *padda-pad, padda-pad* and the *pant-pant-panta-pant* of the wolf had done.

Once more, he kicked up his heels and ran for his life. As he crashed through the wood it seemed to him that something was running with him, keeping pace but never quite showing itself. Something wild and dangerous which could kill him as soon as look at him if it chose.

And then it was gone, whatever it was, and Wilfred was alone again.

Owls hooted – *oo-hoo, oo-hoo* – as if mocking him, and he came to a halt, breathing hard, wishing he was back home, snug in his coffin.

But then he remembered his plan to prove that he was a true vampire and make his father proud of him. He *must* get to the village.

Ah, but which way was the village? With all this mad dashing about, Wilfred had lost all sense of direction. He wandered this way and that for ages, but never came to the end of the wood.

Every now and then there was a movement ahead of him and he changed direction to avoid it. Then, a little later, he would sense a presence in the dark and would swerve again to avoid it.

All of a sudden Wilfred smelt something very unexpected in that haunted wood: roasting meat. He peered through the trees and saw the bright flicker of a campfire. He crept forward till he came to a clearing. In the clearing sat a boy.

The boy, who had his back to Wilfred, sat on a log roasting something over the fire. It was a squirrel, which looked as if it was crisping up nicely. Wilfred realised that he was hungry. Very hungry. He licked his lips. He could almost taste that squirrel.

But then he cursed his luck. He was a vampire. Vampires only eat cooked meat when there's nothing living to sink their teeth into.

He looked again at the boy. He wore a long black cloak with the hood thrown back. An easy matter, Wilfred decided, to sneak up, bite the boy's neck, and sip enough blood to take the edge off his appetite. Then he would squirt some blood into his jug before going on to the village for ...

The jug. Where was it? He looked about him. He couldn't remember dropping it or putting it down, but he no longer had it and that was a fact.

So now what? Perhaps the boy in the clearing had something he could use. He couldn't ask, of course, because some of the blood he planned to take home was going to be the boy's. Perhaps if he drained off just enough to weaken the boy he could find a container, then squirt some more of his blood into it. Good plan!

Wilfred crept across the clearing until he stood behind the boy. He got ready to sink his fangs into his victim's neck. But then the tempting smell of roasting squirrel pinched his nostrils and his knees sagged. Oh, why do I have to be a vampire? he thought. I would so much prefer leg of squirrel to neck of boy.

"So what are you waiting for?"

Wilfred jumped. The boy had spoken and now turned to look up at him.

"It's quite clean, you know," the boy said.

"Wh-what is?" Wilfred stammered.

"My neck. Washed it only last month. But you've missed your chance. You'll have to be quicker than that if you're going to bite me."

"How did you know I was behind you?" Wilfred asked. "How did you know what I was going to do?"

"Eyes in the back of my head," said the boy. "And I tell you, if your teeth had come within a nip of my neck you'd have needed a dentist the next instant. What's it all about? Think you're a vampire, do you?"

Wilfred stepped over the log and faced the boy.

"I don't *think* I'm a vampire. I *am* a vampire. My father is Count Dracula!"

Now this really did take the boy by surprise.

"Count Dracula is your father? But he's my hero! It's because of him that I became a night hunter."

"Night hunter?" Wilfred said.

"Someone who hunts by night. I'm good at it too. Always have been. From the moment I could walk, I wanted to stay out all night and sleep all day like the Count. My parents used to curse the very name Dracula. He set a bad example to young boys, they said."

"Don't your parents mind any more?" asked Wilfred, sitting down on the log.

"Not since the night of the storm, they don't," the boy said.

"What happened the night of the storm?"

"Lightning struck a tree beside the house. It crashed through the roof and flattened them in their sleep. I was out at the time – hunting."

"How sad," said Wilfred.

"Oh, it could be worse. I can go out whenever I want now, no questions asked." He glanced at Wilfred. "What are you called?"

"Wilfred," said Wilfred.

"My name's Smirk," the boy said, smirking. "Like a bit of squirrel? It's about done."

Wilfred shook his head. "I can't. Vampires don't eat cooked meat."

"That's a shame, I prepared it just for you."

"For me?"

"I was expecting you. In fact I guided you here."

"Nobody guided me," Wilfred said. "I just walked through the wood, walked whichever way I wanted."

"Mostly you ran," Smirk said. "And every now and then something made you swerve and go in another direction. That was me."

He tore a leg off the squirrel and offered it to Wilfred. Wilfred was so hungry by this time that he took the leg and, vampire or not, sank his teeth into it.

He rolled his eyes. It was the best thing he'd ever tasted.

He noticed Smirk watching him with amusement. "Aren't you having any?" Wilfred asked.

"No. I have no taste for dead flesh."

As if to prove this, Smirk snatched a mouse as it scurried by and popped it in his mouth. The little hind legs and tail stuck out between his lips, twitching. He crunched hard. The little hind legs and tail went limp. Smirk spat them out and chewed up the rest.

"You dropped this," he said then, and reached down beside him.

Wilfred stared. It was his jug, his own jug, the one he'd lost. "How did you come by this?"

"You dropped it when you climbed the tree to escape the wolf."

"You saw that?" Wilfred said.

"More than saw it. Where do you think the arrow came from?"

"If that was you, then I owe you my life."

"It was and you do," said Smirk. "Eat up now."

Wilfred did so, eagerly. The squirrel was so tasty, and the fire so cheering, that before long he grew quite drowsy.

"Feel free to take a nap," Smirk said.

"I can't. I have to go to the village. There's something I must fetch for my father."

"The night is young. Plenty of time for a nap *and* a trip to the village and back before dawn. Go on, have a little doze, you'll feel better for it."

The idea of a nap appealed to Wilfred. He curled up against a log, and very soon was sleeping like ... well, like a log.

Chapter 4
Smirk's Gift

Wilfred's eyelids felt warm. He opened them, to be almost blinded by sunshine. He flung his arm across his eyes in horror. "The sun! Oh no, the sun!"

Smirk stood nearby, the hood of his cloak pulled up over his head. "It doesn't seem to have done you much harm so far."

Wilfred lowered his arm and to his surprise the sunlight did not affect him. He'd never been out during the day before, so he had never felt the sun on his face, or watched it dance on the back of his hands.

"I don't understand," he said. "Father says daylight is harmful to vampires. And it's even worse when we're older. Then it turns us to dust. All my life he's told me that only normal people can survive during the day. People like you. Boring Normals, he calls you."

"Is this what you call *normal?*" Smirk said.

He tugged the hood back a fraction. His face was as pale as death, his eyes as red as cherry tomatoes. He looked ill. Very, *very* ill.

"I'm allergic to sunlight. It gets worse every year. When I was little, I stayed out at night and indoors between sunrise and sunset to be like the Count. Now I have to, like it or not."

"Why aren't you indoors now, then?"

"Because I wanted to see how the sun would affect a real vampire."

"But it might have done me serious harm," Wilfred said, in horror. "And you would have just stood there *watching*?"

"I was curious," Smirk said, and pulled his hood over his face again. "I've never met an actual vampire before. But the weird thing is, the sun doesn't seem to hurt you at all – unlike me, and I'm just a farmer's son."

Now Wilfred became excited. "Do you realise what this means? It means that all these centuries we Draculas have shut ourselves away in that gloomy, old castle when we could have been out and about. Just think, we could have been chatting to the neighbours, having picnics, boating on the river! I must go and tell Father at once!"

"I thought you had something to do in the village," Smirk said.

"Oh, this is much more important." Wilfred was keen to be off. "Goodbye, Smirk. Thanks for killing the wolf and cooking the squirrel. Perhaps we'll meet again some time."

"Can I come with you?"

"Come with me? No, no. The only visitors Father welcomes are those who want to donate blood. That doesn't include you, I imagine."

"No," said Smirk firmly. "Look, I just want a glimpse of him. I'll make sure he doesn't see me, I promise."

"Even if I agree," Wilfred said, "you don't look well enough to walk all that way."

"Who said anything about walking?"

Smirk raised his arms and his long cloak fluttered about him as if it had a will of its own. Then his feet left the ground.

Wilfred gasped. "Boring Normals aren't supposed to do that! Even I can't do it, and I'm a vampire. Father's tried to show me many times, but I never could get the hang of it."

"I've been able to do it since I was a toddler," Smirk said, "a sort of gift, I suppose, to make up for being allergic to sunlight. Take hold of my cloak."

Wilfred took hold of the cloak and his empty jug, and the next moment he and Smirk were rising through the trees.

Soon, the wood was a bright carpet of leaves beneath them. Wilfred's amazement turned to pleasure. He laughed and glanced at Smirk, but his new friend's face was hidden by the hood of his cloak. For an instant, the hood looked less like a hood than the head of a monstrous bat.

"Are you ready?" Smirk asked.

"Yes," said Wilfred.

"Then off we go!"

The cloak folded about Wilfred, flapped a couple of times like great, black wings, and then they were flying – yes, flying! – towards Castle Dracula.

Chapter 5
A True Vampire

Smirk said nothing more until they drew near the castle. "I've longed to visit this place," he said from deep within his hood. "Never quite found the nerve. Where do we find him, your noble father?"

"He'll be asleep by now," Wilfred said. "That's his coffin-room up there. The window next to the drainpipe."

"The shutters are closed."

"Closed against the light, that's all. They're not locked."

They came to rest on the wide window ledge. Wilfred pushed the shutters back just enough to see in.

"There," he whispered.

Smirk pressed an eye to the crack and saw his great hero snoring gently in his coffin. A shaft of light entered the room by the same crack, and touched the Count's hand.

"He'll be furious if he knows I've brought someone home with me," Wilfred said. "You'd better stay out here."

"Stay out here? You forget, I'm allergic to the sun."

"Oh, all right, go in then. But don't make a sound – and hide yourself."

Wilfred opened the shutters a little more and Smirk jumped in, silent as a cat, and tiptoed across the gloomy room.

While Smirk hid himself behind a heavy curtain, Wilfred also entered. But he was so eager to speak to his father that he left the shutters ajar. The sunlight followed him in as he went over to the coffin and shook the Count gently by the shoulder.

"Father, great news! It's not true that direct sunlight harms vampires. We can go out whenever we want! I've proved it!"

The Count frowned in his sleep. He stirred. His lips drew back to reveal two sharp teeth at the corners of his mouth.

"Who dares disturb my slumbers?" he growled.

"It's me, Wilfred. Come on, Father, wake up. You don't have to sleep during the day any more. Look, I'll show you."

The groggy Count sat up and scratched the back of his hand where the sun had touched it. What nonsense was the boy talking? The sun harmless? Had he lost his mind?

Wilfred ran to the window and flung the shutters wide. Sunshine flooded the room. The Count, elegant in his black silk pyjamas with 'CD' on the top pocket, scrambled out of his coffin in panic.

"Wilfred, what are you doing? Close the shutters!"

"It's all right, Father, don't worry, the light won't hurt you!"

The Count stepped forward, intending to rush at the shutters and slam them shut. But the sun fell full upon him and all energy drained out of him. As the golden glow bathed him from head to foot he drooped, and the wax in his hairy old ears melted and dribbled onto his shoulders.

"Oh, foolish boy!" he wailed, falling back.

Wilfred stared. "But why does the light hurt you and not me? I'm your son, your own flesh and blood. It doesn't make sense."

"But it does," said the Count. "I've suspected it for years, and this proves it. Close the shutters before it's too late. I have something to tell you, Wilfred."

But Wilfred was too excited to think about shutters. "Something to tell me? What, Father, what?"

"Remember the story I used to tell you at coffin-time about when you were a baby and Baron Gertler took the form of a bat and carried you off?"

"Yes, what of it?"

With the sunlight eating into him, the Count grew leaner and more wizened by the second. The skin shrivelled on his cheeks. His jaw stood out like a bent shovel. The bones of his wrists and elbows looked like knotted pipe-cleaners.

"I followed the Baron to a small farm," he said, with some difficulty. "He had a headstart on me, but I saw him carry you into the farmhouse before making his escape through a window. He paid for that night's mischief later. Oh, how he paid!"

The red gleam returned for a moment to his eyes as he remembered how he had defeated his old enemy. But then his eyes dulled once more. He gave a dry cough, and his chest caved in. "The shutters, Wilfred, the shutters."

"Oh, yes. Sorry, Father."

Wilfred slammed the shutters, but so eager was he to hear the rest of the story that he didn't close them properly. As he returned to his father's coffin-side, one of them swung slowly open again and light once more filled half the room – the half where the drooping Count sprawled against his coffin.

"Go on, Father, what happened then?"

"By the time I reached the farmhouse," the Count continued, breathing hard, "the night was almost over. In minutes, the sun would be up and I would be done for. I flew into the house to scoop you up – and came upon a cradle with *two* babies in it."

"Two?" said Wilfred, startled.

The Count's splendid pyjamas turned to rags in the golden light.

"In his haste to escape me," he went on, "the Baron had dropped you in the cradle he found in that room, next to the new child of the house. I had to decide – in great haste – which of the two was mine."

"But surely you knew which was your own *son*," Wilfred said.

"All babies look the same to me," the Count snapped. "I had to make a choice before the sun rose and destroyed me. I seized the one that seemed to have my nose and ... Wilfred, I hate to tell you this, but ..."

"You brought the wrong baby home."

"Seems I did," said the Count.

"So I'm not your son after all?"

"Seems not. Sorry, Wilf."

"Can it be so?" Smirk, the night hunter, stepped out from behind the curtain.

The amazed Count's brittle jaw almost shattered upon his chest.

"Who's this?" he demanded feebly.

"His name's Smirk," Wilfred told him. "We met in Stoker Wood. He saved my life and gave me a leg of roast squirrel. He's a big fan of yours."

"More than a fan, it seems," Smirk said, keeping to the shadows. "My mother often told me that I changed overnight when I was a baby, but she never thought for a moment that I might have been exchanged for her real son."

"Exchanged?" Wilfred said. "You were exchanged for *me*?"

Smirk's eyes were bright red and the teeth at the corners of his mouth looked very sharp. "It explains everything. My allergic reaction to sunlight. The fact that I can fly. My taste for live flesh. I'm not a Boring Normal after all. I never was. I'm the son of Count Dracula himself!"

Chapter 6
Dreams Come True

Risking the dreadful sunlight, Smirk darted from the shadows and hugged the withered old Count.

"Kiss me, Father!"

The hug was too much for the dying vampire. His ribcage cracked in several places. With his last breath he said, "Don't ... squeeze ... please ..."

Then Smirk was holding not a father but two armfuls of really old dust. He opened his arms and the dust fell to the floor. Shocked as he was, he remembered to go back into the shadows before the sun weakened him.

"If you are my father's real son," Wilfred said, wiping a tear from his cheek, "then ... who am I?"

"You," said Smirk, "are the only son of Dweeb van Helsing, the man I grew up calling Papa – or Miseryguts, depending on my mood."

"But he's dead too," Wilfred said sadly. "I'll never even meet him."

"Not unless you dig him up," Smirk replied. "But you have the farm."

"Farm?" said Wilfred.

"It came to me when Mama and Papa were killed. It's a bit of a mess because I never cared for farming myself but you're welcome to it. And I suppose I'd better move in here and become the new Count Dracula. Er ... you don't mind, do you?"

"Mind?" Wilfred cried happily. "This is wonderful! I don't have to prove anything any more. I'm not a vampire. Or even a wimpire. I'm a Boring Normal!"

"And I," said Smirk, "can stop feeling bad about not working in the fields and milking the rotten cows."

"You have cows?" said Wilfred in wonder.

"Five," said Smirk.

"Then I can have fresh milk every morning."

"You can have it till it pours out of your ears. And I, at last, have a good excuse to drink blood."

"I suppose we'll have to swap names too," Wilfred said.

"Let's not," said Smirk. "I don't see myself as a Wilfred somehow."

With these important matters settled between them, they fetched a broom and swept the dust of the late Count into an empty biscuit tin. Smirk put the tin on the mantelpiece in the dining room and made a solemn vow never to put biscuits in it.

Then Wilfred van Helsing, farmer's son, left Castle Dracula for the last time. He sang a cheery song and there was a spring in his step as he strolled down Bram Hill. Ahead of him lay the life he'd always dreamed of. A very ordinary life, in which

he could lie about in the sun all day, and sleep all through the night.

Oh yes, and not feel bad about preferring milk fresh from the cow to blood fresh from the neck.

Young Monsters

by

Michael Lawrence

Illustrated by Chris Mould

For Linda and Ian

Contents

Chapter 1

Sent Away

Lon's father was forever calling him a "young monster". Lon didn't like this at all, but his father was a stern man. To tell the truth, Lon was a bit afraid of him. One day his father said:

"Lon, pack your bags. I'm sending you away."

"Away?" said Lon, nervously.

"To my old boarding school where they know exactly what to do with young monsters like you. I'll be popping in to see how you're getting on and, if I don't see improvements very quickly, I shall be most unhappy."

So Lon was sent off in a pony and trap to his father's old boarding school. As they neared the gates, the pony reared up, almost tipping Lon and the driver out.

"Whoa, boy! Steady, steady!" the driver said. When the pony had settled down, the driver said to Lon: "This is as far as I'm taking you. Old Nell won't go through these gates."

Lon got down from the trap. The driver threw his bag out after him and drove away at speed. Lon stood at the gates of his new school, looking at the big sign beside them.

Suddenly, a sharp voice said: "What is your business here?" The words came from the gates themselves.

"I've been sent to study here," Lon replied.

"Another young monster!" the gates cried, swinging open with a sound like several sharp knives scraping across several dinner plates. "Well come in, come in. If you think I'm going to waste my day talking to you, you're wrong."

Lon passed through the gates. "Thanks very much," he said as they grumbled to a close. He was a polite boy.

At the end of the weed-littered drive there stood an enormous ramshackle house. Reaching the front door, Lon seized the great iron knocker and banged it as hard as he dared. There was a pause. A really long pause, in which there was no sound of any kind. It was the kind of pause that gives a person ... how can I put it? The willies.

But then the door creaked open. Very, very slowly. Very, very creakily. Lon expected to find someone standing on the other side, but there was no one. He went in, and found himself in a massive entrance hall full of cobwebs and shadows and rusty suits of armour.

"H-hello?" he said timidly as the door closed behind him. "Is there anybody here?"

He thought he heard a cackle of laughter. He looked about but, seeing no one, decided he must have imagined it. He did not imagine the large cat that ran at him and sank its sharp little teeth into his ankle, however.

"Eeeeeeyoooowaaaaaaaah!" said Lon (or something rather like it).

The echo of Lon's screech of pain bounced around from wall to wall and up and down the stairs for some time before it got fed up and fell to the floor in a sulk. Another silent willyish pause might have started up then if it had not been for the voice.

"You mustn't mind Tiddles," the voice said. "He loves boys' ankles, that's all."

It was quite a muffled voice, and it seemed to come from a large bowl of fruit on a tall trolley.

"Wh-where are you?" Lon said with a gulp.

"Somewhere between the grapes, the bananas and the rotten apples," the voice replied.

Lon removed some of the fruit and peered into the fruit bowl. There, right in the middle, was a human head.

And it was looking right at him.

Chapter 2
The Head

The head had the brightest blue eyes, the hairiest ginger eyebrows, and the longest teeth that Lon had ever seen.

"Where's the rest of you?" Lon said, with some alarm.

"If you mean my body, well it's a very sad tale. Would you like to hear it?"

"Not really," said Lon.

But the head told him anyway. "I was young and foolish and devil-may-care," he began. "I failed to heed the advice of my monstrous elders and took the bolt from my neck. When my head fell off, my body toppled over a cliff and was torn apart by eagles. Never *ever* remove your bolt, my boy. Look what can happen. Oh, but I see that you have no bolt. Well, we'll soon put that right."

"Who are you?" Lon asked.

"Oh, didn't I say? I'm Dr Ffelix Ffurter, Head of this fine establishment. And your name is ...?"

"Lon, sir. My father sent me here to study."

"Ah yes, our new First Year. Get the rest of this fruit off me, there's a good lad."

"What's all this fruit doing round your head anyway?" Lon asked as he cleared the fruit away.

"I was hiding," the Head answered. "Hiding my head under a pile of fruit not only allows me to keep an eye on the general comings and goings, but the vitamin C is good for my chin. Step this way, young fellow!"

The trolley whizzed round and rattled away, with the Head bobbing around on top of it. Lon followed. They came to a large door.

"Open!" the Head commanded.

The door flew back angrily, as if it would prefer to stay shut, or write a poem, or do something else entirely. The trolley shot inside and wheeled itself behind a big leather-topped desk. The Head peered across the desk at Lon.

"I see very little of the monster in you, boy," he said. "But your father wouldn't have sent you here if he didn't think there was *something* monstrous about you."

"No one thought me very monstrous at my last school," Lon informed him. "In fact, I was quite popular there."

"What sort of school was it?" the Head asked.

"Oh, just an ordinary one. Very different from here."

As he said this, Lon swept his arm around the room. Sadly, the Head's study was very cluttered and Lon's sweeping arm sent a vase of dead flowers flying. The vase struck a large mirror, and the mirror shattered and fell to the floor in pieces. One of the pieces just missed Tiddles the cat, who had followed them, hoping for a nip at Lon's other ankle.

"A broken mirror," Dr Ffurter said cheerfully. "Another seven years' bad luck! Hmm, perhaps you're more of a monster than you look. You work hard, my boy, and in a year or two you might be ready to sit your GCME exam."

"My what?" Lon asked.

"The General Certificate of Monstrous Excellence. But first things first." He raised his voice, "Mrs Staines!"

There was a grumpy sigh from across the room, and the ghostly shape of a bad-tempered crone leaned out of a panel in the wall.

"Is there no peace even in *death*?" snapped the old woman.

"Mrs Staines," said the Head to his ghostly secretary, "please be so good as to call a student. I have need of one."

Mrs Staines opened her mouth wide enough to swallow a football and screamed the most ear-splitting scream Lon had ever heard.

"Why is she screaming?" he cried.

"It's her way of calling boys," Dr Ffurter explained. "If the nearest boy doesn't hammer at my door within six seconds of that scream, he knows that Mrs Staines and a bunch of her horrible dead relatives will haunt him till the end of term."

Five and a half seconds after the scream had died away, there was a hammering at the door. "Come in!" bawled the Head.

The door flew open. A boy stood there. A scowling, green-faced boy with freckles and fangs. He had a hammer in his hand and a large bolt through his neck.

"Ah, Grout," said the Head. "I would like you to escort our new student here to Matron to have his bolt fitted. When she's done with him, show him the way to Dormitory Six, where a bed full of crushed cockroaches awaits him."

Grout replaced his hammer in the holster at his hip. "Right you are, sir." Then he grabbed Lon's left ear and hauled it out of the room. You may not be surprised to learn that Lon followed quite closely behind.

Chapter 3
Grout

Now Lon was a sweet-tempered lad, but every so often he saw red. Seeing red, as you probably know, means getting really annoyed. Lon saw red as Grout dragged him along the corridor by his left ear. (He would have been just as annoyed if it had been his right ear, but that's by the way.)

"Let me go!" he shouted, trying to wriggle out of Grout's loutish grip.

"Not a chance," Grout said, with a grin so wide and sloppy that drool dribbled from the corners of his mouth. "I've decided I don't like you. You look much too normal to me."

The building was very old and gloomy, with cobwebs drooping from every corner and rats scampering at every turn. Grout brought his foot down on the tail of one of the rats. The tail remained while the rat made its escape. Grout scooped up the tail and lowered it slowly into his mouth like a strand of freshly-cooked spaghetti. "Tasty," he said, slapping his lips.

When they reached Matron's room, Grout took out his hammer and banged on the door.

"Why don't you use your knuckles?" Lon said, twisting and turning in the bigger boy's grip.

Grout squeezed his ear even harder. "I save my knuckles for First Years," he said. "Besides, knocking on doors with your knuckles is what normal people do. I'm not normal. I'm a young monster."

"You don't say," said Lon.

The door opened into a small, cave-like room containing a single high bed. On the bed sat a boy of about Lon's age. Like Grout, and every other boy they'd passed on the way, the boy had a large bolt through his neck. A plump woman with tufty warts was looking through the boy's hair. Her nose was running, Lon noticed, though the rest of her stayed where it was.

"No," Matron said to the boy. "No lice. Not a single one. You'll really have to work harder to attract them, Omar. Down you get." The boy slipped down from the bed and Matron turned to Lon and Grout. "Now, what can I do for you two?"

Grout yanked Lon's ear towards the bed. "New kid for you, Matron. The Head sent him to—"

He was going to add, "... have his bolt fitted", but just then Lon fell over Tiddles, the school cat, who had been trying to trip one of them up all the way from the Head's study. Lon's elbow flew back and struck Grout on the nose. Grout yelped. Blood spurted. Unlike most boys' blood, Grout's was green. It was also rather thick and sticky, like treacle (but probably not quite so nice on pancakes).

Lon tried to regain his balance but, as he did so, his head came up under Grout's chin. Grout yelped again and hit the floor.

Lon hadn't meant these things to happen, of course, and he was sorry about them. Full of apology, he leant down to help Grout up but, to his horror, Grout's hand came away!

"Eergh!" he shouted, and flung Grout's hand away from him. As it hurtled across the room, the hand became a fist and it struck the monster-fish tank under the window, smashing it to smithereens. Suddenly, the floor was awash with monster-fish, all bulgy eyes and snappy little teeth. Tiddles ran for his life.

Grout's hand, meanwhile, seemed to be practising dance steps on the window ledge. It might have been quite happy to go on doing this for some time if it hadn't slipped. Over the ledge it went, down and down and down, until it came to rest in the jaws of Russ, the school dog. Russ had three heads and three sets of jaws which each gulped down a share of Grout's hand before you could say *Woof!*

"My favourite hand!" wailed Grout from the window.

"Don't worry," Matron said. "We'll dig up a new one for you."

"It won't be the same. I loved that hand. It was my grandpa's." Grout turned on Lon. "I'll get you for this, new kid!"

Lon tried to tell him that it had been an accident, but Grout refused to listen. He charged out of the room, swearing to make Lon pay for feeding his grandpa's hand to the dog.

Chapter 4
Bolted

The boy without the head lice didn't believe it had been an accident either, and he was impressed at the way Lon had dealt with Grout. "Pleased to meet you," he said. "My name's Omar." He held out his hand. Lon eyed it with suspicion. "Don't worry," Omar said, "it won't come off. I'm not much of a monster. I'm a great let down to my father," he added sadly.

"So am I to mine," said Lon.

"Now, why did the Head send you to me?" Matron asked Lon.

"Tell her it was for some ointment for his You-Know-What," Omar whispered to Lon.

"What's his You-Know-What?" Lon whispered back.

"I've no idea, but I've heard him mention it to Matron. And pull your collar up. Don't let her see your neck, whatever you do."

Lon pulled his collar up and turned to Matron. "He sent me to ask for some ointment for his You-Know-What."

"But I only gave him some on Friday," Matron said in surprise.

"He must have used it all up," Lon replied, wishing he knew what he was talking about.

Matron gave him a tub of ointment for the Head. The label said:

You-Know-What Ointment. Keep out of reach of children and DON'T SWALLOW!

Outside, Lon said: "Why did I have to lie to her?"

"I'm guessing that the Head sent you to have a bolt fitted," Omar said.

"Yes, he did. What is all this bolt stuff anyway?"

"At normal boarding schools boys have to wear ties," Omar explained. "At monster schools they wear bolts through their necks instead. Some kids come with their bolts already fitted, like Grout and his pals. They've had them since they were toddlers. The rest of us are bolted as soon as we arrive."

"Was your bolt fitted before or after you arrived?" Lon asked him.

"Neither," Omar said. "I fooled them. 'Once bolted, always bolted.' I didn't want that. Do you want that?"

"Not really, now you mention it. But won't they notice if I don't have a bolt?"

"Not if you put this on." Omar dipped into his pocket and pulled out a strap-on bolt. "It's my spare. You can have it. I'll write to my mum for another. She's not keen on bolting. It's my father who wants me to be a monster. He says it's the only way to get on in this world."

Omar strapped the bolt onto Lon's neck. It looked just like the real thing.

"That boy Grout was supposed to show me to Dormitory Six," Lon said. "Any idea which way it is?"

"That's my dorm," Omar said with pleasure. "Come on, I'll take you."

They set off through the long, gloomy corridors. "You've made an enemy of Grout," he said as they walked. "Rather you than me. Keep looking over your shoulder, that's my advice."

They climbed flight after flight of shadowy stairs. There were cobwebby shelves all the way up containing skulls, jars of eyeballs like gobstoppers and heaps of grinning teeth.

"I don't really know what monster schools are for," Lon said. "I should, because my father works for the Institute of Monster Education. But he never talks about his work and I never ask. Isn't monstrous behaviour frowned upon in the outside world?"

"Dr Ffurter says that monsters play an important role in society," Omar informed him. "He says that if humans aren't frightened now and then by nightmare creatures, they have trouble dealing with the boring routines of normal life."

There were several boys in Dormitory Six when they got there. All had bolts through their necks. Some also had huge eyes, or extra arms and legs, or were

extremely hairy. Some growled, some looked frightening, some looked plain silly. But a few of them seemed so normal that Lon was puzzled.

"They might *look* normal," Omar whispered, "but no one is sent here unless his parents think he's a young monster. It doesn't always show, that's all."

"You look pretty normal too, come to that," Lon said.

Omar seemed rather upset by this. "I do try," he said. "Look." He pulled his worst monster face. Lon chuckled. "No, no, no," said Omar. "It's meant to be scary, not funny!"

"I wasn't laughing," Lon said, hiding his grin. "I was shaking with terror."

This cheered Omar up. It was good to have a friend.

Chapter 5
The Task

Next morning, all students and teachers were called to the main hall, where Dr Ffurter had some news which seemed to upset him.

"I have just received word that the School Spectre is coming tomorrow," he announced. "He's going to poke into every nook and cranny, assess your monstrous progress and write a report on us."

He was so agitated that he turned into a werewolf, jumped to the ground and howled at the moon that wasn't out yet.

"The Head's off his trolley," Lon said to Omar.

"He'll get back on it in a minute," Omar said. He was right. The werewolf jumped up onto the trolley and became the Head again.

"This school looks far too normal," the Head said. "We must tidy it down. Make it look quite disgraceful. I will order a fresh batch of skeletons and some more tarantulas and rats – *please* don't snack on the rats between meals, boys – and I expect every student to be on his worst behaviour while the Spectre is here."

"Can we spit in his eye?" one boy yelled out.

"I insist that you do," the Head replied. "If the Spectre thinks you aren't monstrous enough, he might close us down and send you to boring, normal schools, where I believe they teach you not to drop litter, cheek your elders, or fiddle with your bottoms in public. How would you like *that* then?"

Some of the boys groaned to show how little they would like it.

"So," the Head went on, "each class will be given specific tasks, and I want you all to get to work at once and do your worst. This school must look and smell as foul as possible. Do I make myself clear?"

Lon and Omar went to their class with the rest of their year. Their class tutor was Professor Bloodless. "Your task, First Years," the Professor said, "is to go into the Wild and collect as many toads and slugs as you can to put in teachers' cups to make them sick. Boys who return empty-handed will be made to tuck their shirts in for a week. Off you go now!"

Grout, who was not a First Year, had been listening outside the door. *So*, he thought, *these kids are going into the Wild, are they?* That gave him an idea. A plan for getting even with Lon for throwing his grandpa's hand to the dog.

Chapter 6
Into the Wild

The Wild, as you might expect, was not a very welcoming place. Trees were tall and twisty, rocks were rough and ready, and the stagnant streams were stinky.

The students were sent off in pairs, with lunch boxes and sacks. The sacks were for the toads and slugs they were to collect. But it wasn't just toads and slugs that lived in the Wild. Far from it. The Wild was full to bursting with monsters of every shape and kind. When some of the First Years came across these dreadful creatures, they found it very hard not to tremble and howl and run back to school shouting, "Mama!"

Lon and Omar certainly met *their* fair share of monsters. They ran into red-eyed ogres, hungry for tasty boy meat. They hid from snarling hellhounds and hissing wildcats. They ducked to avoid great birds with beaks like chain saws and wings like garden spades. There were snakes with poisonous fangs, demons with dodgy horns, and headless horsemen on headless horses. Think of any monster or horror you like, and it was there in the Wild.

But the two boys still managed to find thirteen toads and fifteen slugs, which they put into separate bags so the toads wouldn't eat the slugs, or the slugs cover the toads with slime.

Towards the middle of the afternoon, a heavy mist fell and most of the First Years returned to the school. Lon and Omar might have returned too if they hadn't strayed deeper into the Wild than most and got lost. It was dangerous walking around out there when it was foggy, so they sheltered in a cave.

They lit a fire to keep warm and settled down to wait for the fog to lift. They drew their cloaks about them, and removed the strap-on bolts from their necks. They were much more comfortable without the bolts.

The fog did not lift. As misty afternoon gave way to misty night, Lon and Omar heard, imagined or felt all manner of spooky things: owls hooting, wings brushing their hair, creatures scuffling around them. Once they heard someone calling. They peered nervously into the fog, and saw a dead shepherd calling his dead sheep home.

Around midnight, a bat appeared in the mouth of the cave. The bat grew in size and became a tall, thin man in a cape even blacker than the night.

"Are you a vampire?" asked Lon, trying to sound bold.

"I am," hissed the tall, thin man. "And I'm looking for blood. Shall I take yours, perhaps?"

"We'd rather you didn't," Lon said. "It helps keep us warm on a night like this."

"Aren't you afraid that I might take it, anyway?"

"Of course. But you have kind eyes, so I don't think you will."

The vampire was horrified. "Kind eyes? I've never been so insulted in my death! I wouldn't take your blood if it was the last drop on earth!" He turned back into a bat and flew away.

Chapter 7
Horror of Horrors

Lon and Omar must have fallen asleep at some point because they woke up at another. When they woke it was just after seven in the morning, although they had no way of knowing this. The fog had cleared enough for them to see four hideous creatures, with eyes as red as chilli peppers, lumbering towards the cave mouth.

These four were as terrifying to behold as their moans were terrifying to hear.

Their faces, which looked like withered pumpkins, gave off a faint yellow glow. Their teeth were like pencil stubs. Their feet had six toes each, every one of them the size and colour of a bruised banana.

Lon gulped. "I feel a scream coming on," he said.

"That's nothing," said Omar. "I've just wet myself."

They were about to throw themselves into one another's terrified arms when a rabbit hopped by the cave. It was an ordinary fluffy rabbit with a dear little tail and dear little ears; the kind of rabbit which, at any other time, the two boys would have been delighted to cuddle and stroke while saying, "Aaaah", in soppy voices.

The four advancing creatures did not seem to find the rabbit cuddly, however.

Seeing it hopping merrily by, they threw their arms in the air and shrieked like nobody's business. And as they shrieked dreadful things happened to them.

Their banana toes dropped off.

Their pencil-stub teeth fell out.

Their pumpkin heads fell apart.

It was then that Lon and Omar saw these monsters for what they really were – four boys from Dr Ffurter's: Grout and his pals, Spook, Spittle and Clive, who, to Lon's surprise, lifted their bare feet and ran for it, screaming.

"You know, this time next year we'll be running from rabbits too," said Omar.

"We will?" said Lon. "Why?"

"When young monsters turn twelve they stop liking cuddly things, and start to fear them. You didn't know that?"

"Ssh!" Lon said suddenly. "Quiet!"

He pointed to a fearsome beast dragging its monstrous shadow across the misty cave entrance. The two boys pressed back against the wall. Was this another practical joker, or a true beast of the Wild? But then the flickering light from their

small fire caught the monster's face and
they knew that it was no joker.

"We have to get out of here," Lon whispered. "Quick, while he's looking the other way."

Omar had no idea why his friend was so afraid of this particular beast, but he didn't want to be left in the cave by himself. Grabbing their sacks of jumping toads and slithering slugs, the boys sneaked out of the cave and ran for it.

As they ran, helter-skelter and willy-nilly, terrible creatures stepped out to try and catch them. Jaws reared open to gobble them up. Bloodshot eyes rolled like bloody marbles. Mean claws reached for them. They escaped all of these horrors, but only just, running on and on and on without the faintest idea where they were going.

At last, they came to a high, old wall with a gap in it. They knew as well as you do that gaps in walls are meant to be climbed through, and through they went. And on the other side, they saw ...

"School!" cried Omar with relief.

A downstairs window was open and they clambered in, very glad indeed to be back. They started up the back stairs to their dormitory. But ...

"Oh no!"

... suddenly they found their way blocked by Grout and his three pals – who did not look pleased to see them.

Chapter 8
The School Spectre

"Get lost then, did we?" Grout said. "Ah, poor diddums."

"At least we didn't run screaming from dear little bunny rabbits," Lon replied, but quietly.

"Hey, where are your bolts?" asked Spittle.

Lon and Omar clutched their necks. They'd left their bolts in the cave!

"We took them out," Omar said. "You should try it sometime. It's much more comfortable without them."

"You can't take your bolt out," said Spook. "Remove your bolt and your head falls off, everyone knows that. 'Once bolted, always bolted.'"

"It's not true," Lon said. "Try it – if you dare."

Grout, Spook, Spittle and Clive frowned at one another, not at all sure about this.

"What's up?" said Omar. "Scared?"

"Of course they are," Lon said. "Anyone who's terrified of fluffy little bunnies would be scared of taking his bolt out. Some monsters!"

"Scared?" growled Grout. "I'll show you who's scared!"

He started struggling one-handed with his bolt. His three friends, not wanting to seem scared either, followed his example. The bolts weren't easy to unscrew. They'd been in their necks for most of their lives and were only oiled on leap years.

"Need a hand?" Lon said to Grout, who was having even more trouble getting his bolt out than the others.

Bright green with rage, Grout yanked his bolt so hard with his single hand that it flew out. His pals managed to unscrew theirs at about the same time. Then the four stood grinning at one another.

"It's true," said Clive. "Unbolted heads don't fall off."

Grout sneered at Lon and Omar. "Scared, were we?"

But then, to the four boys' surprise, (but not to Lon and Omar's) their heads tipped slowly forward, hit the floor, and started bouncing down the stairs.

The four headless boys on the landing sat down in shock. "Help!" wailed their heads from the stairs below. "Put our bolts back!"

"I don't hear the magic word," Lon said.

"What magic word?" said Grout's head from the fifth step down.

"The one that starts with 'pl' and ends with 'ease'."

"Please," begged the bouncing heads of Grout and the others, "please, please, *please* put our bolts back!"

"What's in it for us?" said Omar.

"Put our bolts back and we won't play any more jokes on you or bully you ever again," said Grout's head.

"That doesn't sound much to me," Lon said. "Does it sound much to you, Omar?"

"No," said Omar. "Doesn't sound worth the bother to me."

"Wait," said Grout's head from step nine. "We ... we'll bring you breakfast in bed on trays every Sunday. How's that?"

Lon and Omar laughed with delight. "It's a deal!"

They went down and gathered up the four heads and bolted them back into place. They bolted Grout's head on the wrong way round until he complained.

"What I don't understand," Grout said when his head was on properly, "is why your heads don't fall off. Only thing I can think of is that you're not real monsters."

"Careful," Lon said. "You have to be nice to us from now on."

"Grrr," said Grout. Being nice to these two was going to be the hardest thing he'd ever done. Grout and his monstrous gang wandered away, jerking their necks this way and that to make sure their heads were firmly fixed.

Suddenly, there was a mighty knocking at the main door in the hall below. As usual, the door creaked open all by itself. Lon and Omar peered through the banister rails to see who the visitor was.

It was the terrifying creature they had run from at the cave!

"Tell the Head the School Spectre's here," the creature snapped at no one at all.

"Did you hear that?" Omar whispered. "He's the School Spectre!"

"I know," said Lon, crouching in the shadows.

"You know? Is that why you didn't want him to see you in the cave?"

"Sort of."

Down in the hall, the Head's trolley zoomed into sight. "Delighted to see you again, Spectre!" he cried. "Care to join me in my study for a nice glass of warm blood before you tour the school? I have an excellent vintage, from the Dead Sea area. Or perhaps you would prefer a nice tumbler of iced mucus?"

On the Head's orders, the school had been turned upside down and more horrors added everywhere. Bandaged mummies were propped up in corridors. Ghosts swung from broken chandeliers. Skeletons sat in old chairs. Dozens of extra cobwebs dangled from beams. Windows were cracked, doors were off their hinges, potted palms had been treated with rat poison, and so on.

"It's certainly an improvement on last time," the Spectre said when the Head showed him round. "I hoped it would be, seeing as I've just sent my own son here."

Lon and Omar's class of First Years, with the help of their teacher, Professor Bloodless, had prepared a series of surprises for the Spectre. When he was shown into the classroom a bucket of frogspawn fell on his head. Then he slipped on the floor they had greased with oil from a gorgon's armpit. Finally they took out their catapults and pelted him with paper pellets soaked in toilet water.

The Spectre dried his face with a cloth covered in soot, which one of the boys had handed him. "Top of the class, young monsters," he said, "I'm sure you'll do very well at Dr Ffurter's." The Head winked at Professor Bloodless. All was well. The Spectre wouldn't close the school down after what he'd seen today.

Just as he was about to leave, the Spectre whispered something in the Head's ear. The Head called Lon out.

"They've noticed your bolts are missing," Grout hissed as Lon went by. "You're for it now."

Lon pulled his collar up and followed the School Spectre and the Head out of the

room. In the corridor the Spectre asked Dr Ffurter to leave them for a moment, then turned his dreadful gaze on Lon.

"Well, young monster, and how are you finding it?" he asked.

"Could be worse, I suppose," Lon answered.

"It's not easy being monstrous," the Spectre said. "You have to work at it."

"I know," said Lon.

Suddenly, the Spectre plunged his hand into his pocket and pulled out the two strap-on neck bolts that Lon and Omar had left in the cave. "I think these might belong to you," he said.

Lon fixed one of the strap-on bolts round his neck.

"When I next see you, Lon," the Spectre said sternly, "I expect you to be much nastier and uglier than this. I want to be scared out of my wits by you. Is that understood?"

Lon sighed. He had quite a task ahead of him. It wasn't going to be easy, but he had no choice.

"I'll do my best, Father," he said. "Promise."